BOWSER SAVES THE DAY

Jane Misheloff, PhD

Cover Art by
Jo Kosmides Edwards

 ARCHWAY
PUBLISHING

Archway Publishing books may be ordered through booksellers or by contacting:

Archway Publishing
1663 Liberty Drive
Bloomington, IN 47403
www.archwaypublishing.com
1 (888) 242-5904

ISBN: 978-1-4808-8041-2 (sc)
ISBN: 978-1-4808-8052-8 (e)

Library of Congress Control Number: 2019908932

Print information available on the last page.

Archway Publishing rev. date: 07/22/2019

Once again, to all
the wonderful volunteers
at
Mutt Love Rescue

Prologue

If you have at some time or other experienced the loss of a pet dog, you felt sad over that loss whether it was caused by old age, illness, or accident. No doubt you have also wondered, *Where is my dog now? Will I ever see him or her again?*

Here is an opportunity for you to imagine how your dog lives once he or she crosses the Rainbow Bridge. While there are many options available, Les Maisons is a special community where all are welcome in peace and love. Many dogs go there to catch up with their beloved owners already in residence, while others wait patiently for them. It is a comfort to think that your cherished dog is there in such a place surrounded by caring friends and family.

Let's review for a minute.

In *Bowser Becomes the Boss*, we learned that Bowser was a twice-rescued dog that liked to be the boss of his humans and his surroundings. After Bowser crossed the Rainbow Bridge one night, his first rescuer, Helga, joined him one month later. Together, they found a place to live that they named Les Maisons. Soon Bowser and Helga were joined by Coco and Sheila, who had learned about Les Maisons through the dog rescue network. As other dogs joined them, Les Maisons grew by leaps and bounds with beautiful condos, tennis courts, a golf course, and a bone-shaped swimming pool.

Eventually, some dogs who liked to work and keep busy took on specific tasks. Battie liked to bake, so he opened Battie's Bagel Shop. Coco became the concierge. Duffy ran the golf pro shop, and Prima shared some of Duffy's space with ladies' fashions. This group formed Les Maisons's board of directors, with Bowser as its chief bark officer. Helga and Sheila remained as consultants.

In *Bowser Becomes the Boss*, Bowser and his board spent a lot of their time helping newcomers to Les Maisons adjust to their new lives. Ralph, who couldn't walk well before crossing the Rainbow Bridge, kept to himself and ran through the woods alone every day. Bowser introduced him to Duffy, who made Ralph head groundskeeper of the golf course. Darryl longed to sleep in bed with someone, so the board members asked Sheila if she would be willing to share her bed with him. Sheila agreed to the new arrangement. Finally, Prima acquired a new friend, Macy, who loved to shop as much as she did.

In *Bowser the Saves the Day*, we learn about more happenings at Les Maisons, including some mischief on one Saturday night.

Here are two
stories about
newcomers
Henry and Lucky
to Les Maisons—

When Henry crossed the Rainbow Bridge, his bags were full of seed catalogs. His friends wondered what was going on, although they had a sneaking suspicion. They knew Henry's passion—cucumbers!

That evening at his welcome party, Henry was preoccupied with his catalogs. No one could understand why he did not want to join the festivities.

The next day, Henry sent off his seed orders. He waited impatiently every morning for their delivery.

While Henry was waiting for his seeds, Bowser and Coco helped him find a good location for his garden.

Finally, Henry's seeds arrived in the mail. He immediately set to work. He carefully tilled the soil and planted his seeds.

A few weeks later, everyone was surprised to see that all Henry had planted were cucumber seeds. Henry wanted to share his love of cucumbers. However, no one else at Les Maisons knew much about them. Poor Henry's retirement passion did not seem successful.

The Les Maisons board of directors tried to comfort Henry. Helga and Sheila brought love, Prima gave Henry a custom shirt, and Battie brought a tray of bagels. Coco produced a comfy pillow, and Darryl invited Henry to play a round of golf. Bowser took notes.

Bowser had an idea. He conferred with Battie, and they hatched a plan. Invitations were sent out.

Battie got busy in the kitchen while Prima set the tables.

At the special dinner, everybody liked the food so much that they ate it all up. They dined unaware on cucumber: gazpacho soup, fried pickles with spicy mango, Japanese-style pickled cucumbers with seaweed and sesame, and cucumber-nut bread, and they drank honeydew-cucumber slushies. It wasn't until later in the evening that they discovered *all* the dishes they liked so much were made with cucumbers.

When everyone realized what they had been missing, poor Henry could hardly keep up with demand. That did not bother Henry; he was more than happy to share his love of cucumbers with others.

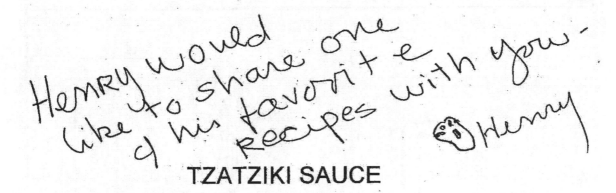

Henry would like to share one of his favorite recipes with you. ☺Henry

TZATZIKI SAUCE

YIELD: 3 CUPS

PREP TIME: 10 MINUTES

TOTAL TIME: 10 MINUTES

INGREDIENTS:

- 2 cups plain Greek yogurt
- 1 cup diced seedless cucumber
- 2 tablespoons fresh lemon juice
- 2 garlic cloves, minced
- 2 tablespoons finely chopped fresh dill
- Salt and pepper, to taste

DIRECTIONS:

1. In a medium bowl, combine Greek yogurt, cucumber, lemon juice, garlic, and dill. Stir until well combined. Taste and season with salt and pepper. If you have time, chill before serving.

Serve with vegetables, pita bread, crackers, falafel, meat, fish or spread on one of Battie's bagels.

Will keep in the refrigerator 2-3 days. Stir before serving.

A poor emaciated little stray beagle appeared one day on Dee's doorstep.

Dee took the pup inside, fed him, and called her dog rescue friends. At first, he suffered from seizures, but as time went on, he became a handsome, outgoing, and friendly little beagle. His rescuers called him Lucky because he was so lucky to be rescued.

Lucky loved everyone, especially the ladies, and one in particular named Gayle.

No matter where Lucky went, if he wanted attention, he would bark loudly.

While in foster care with Debbie and Bill, Lucky was diagnosed with congenital heart failure. The veterinarian also feared he was losing his eyesight.

In his forever home with Pat and Dan, Lucky's health issues never prevented him from enjoying life. He charmed everyone, loved his backyard, made friends with his forevers' other dogs, and shared his food and bed with strangers.

Lucky's heart finally gave out on him. His rescuers, fosters, and forevers came to see him off as he began his climb over the Rainbow Bridge. Lucky turned around to wave back at all those who had loved him.

When Lucky was almost at the end of his journey, he realized he could see again. And to his surprise, there was his old friend Henry waiting for him. Lucky ran into Henry's paws. Henry welcomed Lucky to Les Maisons and introduced him to the board of directors.

Lucky was so happy he could see that he wanted to do everything. He liked swimming in the pool and also took up ballroom dancing.

Duffy coached Lucky into becoming a champion golfer. Most of all, Lucky liked to work with Henry in his cucumber garden.

Sometimes Lucky liked to sit by the reflecting pool in the woods and remind himself that he was one truly lucky dog. He'd had a poor start but a great ending.

Sometimes Mischief making does not end well!

It was Saturday night, and Bowser was tired. He went to bed early and turned off his cell phone.

Helga and her friends went to the opera house to enjoy a performance of *The Valkyries*.

Sheila was at her Saturday-night bridge game, and she made a mental note never to play with Butch again.

Coco, Duffy, Battie, and Prima went to cheer on the Les Maisons championship hockey team at the sports arena.

In the meantime, across town, Mr. Finn's was a popular place on Saturday nights.

On this particular Saturday night, some residents of Les Maisons were behaving badly.

Eventually, Mr. Finn lost his patience and showed the mischief-makers to the door.

Several of the merrymakers proceeded to the nearby railway tracks, where they commenced to dance Irish jigs.

The police came soon enough and urged the dogs to leave the area immediately for their own safety.

The dogs dallied. No member of the board of directors at Les Maisons could be reached, so the police decided to take everyone to the police station until a responsible party could come and pick them up.

Bowser to the Rescue—

When Bowser learned the following morning what had happened, he led a golf cart caravan to the police station to bring the miscreants home.

Mr. Finn was also busy back at P. Finn's Fine Food.

Bowser called an emergency meeting of the Les Maisons board of directors. He asked them for recommendations so such incidents would not happen again. The board decided on two steps.

The first step called for two weeks of community service for those involved in improper behavior at Mr. Finn's and at the railroad tracks.

The second step called for all residents of Les Maisons to attend etiquette lessons taught by Prima and her assistant, Marilyn, on table manners and proper restaurant behavior.

However, after two weeks of begging and pleading by everyone, Bowser agreed to meet with Mr. Finn to see whether he would relent and allow Les Maisons dogs to go there on Saturday nights if they behaved themselves.

After he heard Bowser's deal, Mr. Finn agreed to let Les Maisons dogs come back on Saturday nights.

The world-famous Jeb's Beagles Kentucky Bluegrass Band would play two sets every Saturday night.

Popular dancers Billy and Nadia would conduct square dance lessons in the second-floor lounge every Tuesday night, traditionally a slow night.

Now everyone could come to P. Finn's restaurant on Saturday nights to enjoy dinner while waiting for Jeb's Kentucky Bluegrass Band to play their first set.

The next morning all the dogs circled Bowser to show their thanks by giving him high fours. Helga was proud of Bowser as usual.

On his way home, Bowser stopped at one of his favorite spots to reflect what *Les Maisons* meant to him and so many others.

The End

Bowser hopes that you enjoyed reading about the pups at Les Maisons.

Printed in the United States
By Bookmasters